The WOMBAT

by Pauline Reilly

illustrated by Will Rolland

Kangaroo Press

The information in this book is based on *The Common Wombat* by Barbara Triggs (in press) and on papers by Graham Brown and Greg Young of CSIRO Wildlife & Rangelands Research. We thank all three for their unstinting assistance, especially Barbara Triggs, who generously supplied reference photographs.

© Pauline Reilly (text) and Will Rolland (illustrations) 1987

Reprinted 1989, 1990, 1991, 1992, 1994, 1995 and 1998
First published 1988 by Kangaroo Press
an imprint of Simon & Schuster Australia
20 Barcoo Street, East Roseville NSW 2069
Printed in Singapore by Kyodo Printing Co (S'pore) Pte Ltd

ISBN 0 86417 148 X

It was wombat time, the time of day when
wombats come out of their burrows.
The sun was setting and shadows were long.

A baby wombat poked her head out
of her mother's pouch and looked at the world.
She was six months old.
For the first four months of her life, she had
lived inside the pouch, always with a teat
in her mouth to drink her mother's milk.

4

Now when the mother wombat stopped to graze,
the baby wombat leaned out of the pouch and
nibbled pieces of grass.
Then she turned around
and dropped her droppings outside.

Inside the burrow, the baby climbed out of the pouch.
She was furry all over.
She played with her mother
in the nursery chamber lined with bracken and soft bark.

She waddled slowly up and down the tunnels.
Then she climbed back into the pouch and
snuggled down. Lying on her back, she took
a teat in her mouth before falling asleep.

She began to dig her own tunnels inside the burrow,
pushing out the dirt with all four paws
when she backed out again.

The mother wombat kicked the earth out of
the burrow entrance where it made a large mound.

When the young wombat was ten months old,
she had grown too big for the pouch.

She trotted along behind her mother...

...or played, leaping into the air,

bounding up a slope,

rolling down slowly,

over and over and over.

Half a year later, the mother wombat
no longer wanted her young one in her feeding ground.
The time had come for the young wombat
to find a feeding ground of her own.
She wandered away.

A dead wombat that had been hit by a car lay beside a road.
She sniffed the dead wombat.
Then, still sniffing, she found its feeding ground
and claimed it for herself.

She found a burrow underneath the root of a tree.
But when it rained, water seeped in.

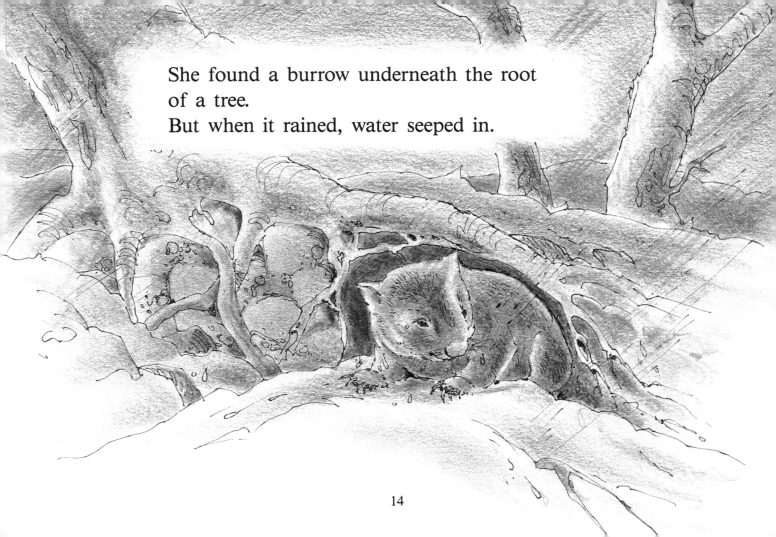

She dug herself another burrow under a rock.
But there were rocks inside and she could not
make it deep enough.

So she dug another and this one was good.

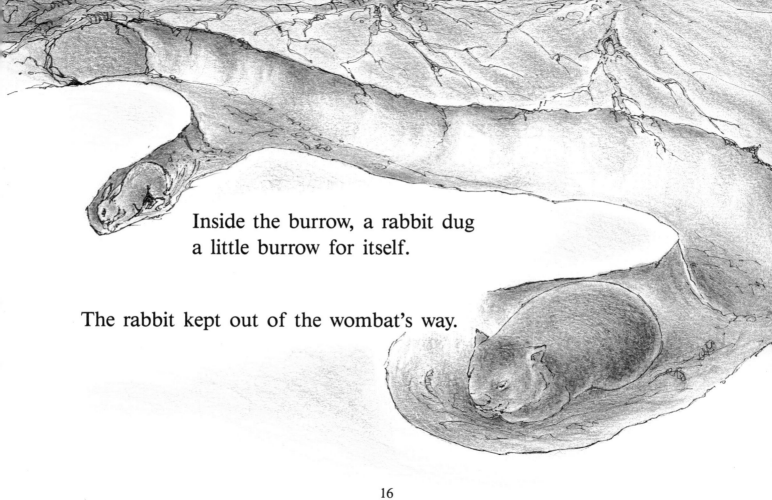

Inside the burrow, a rabbit dug
a little burrow for itself.

The rabbit kept out of the wombat's way.

To keep her coat clean and to get rid of ticks and mites and fleas, the young wombat scratched with all four feet one after the other.

She chose her own rubbing posts
so that she could scratch her back when it itched.

After scratching the ground, she placed
her droppings on rocks or raised earth
or logs, but never inside a burrow.

These droppings and rubbing posts
acted as landmarks to help her find her way
and to show other wombats that this home range was occupied.

In hot weather, she stayed deep down
in the burrow where the temperature was
always comfortable.

      She lay quietly and rested until
the weather became cooler.

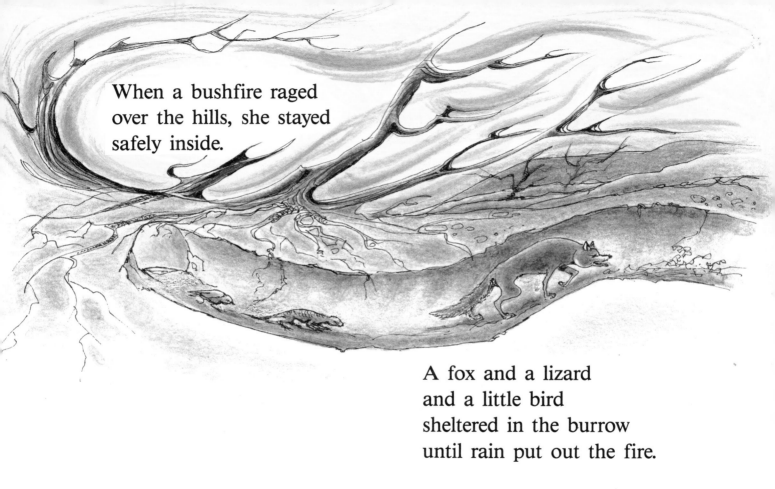

When a bushfire raged
over the hills, she stayed
safely inside.

A fox and a lizard
and a little bird
sheltered in the burrow
until rain put out the fire.

After the fire, she had to walk further to find food.
She dug out the roots of little plants and ate the leaves of rushes.
This tough and wiry food ground down her teeth
but they kept growing from underneath and never became shorter.

Water was not a problem because she drank
only when her food was dry.

Sometimes on cloudy days, she went outside
before night fell and sat near the burrow entrance.
From here she knew when danger threatened
and could go back into her burrow.

One dull, dark day in winter,
she dug her way through the snow
over her burrow.
Her thick skin and furry coat
kept out the cold.

Looking for food under the snow, she ambled up a hill and slid down the other side

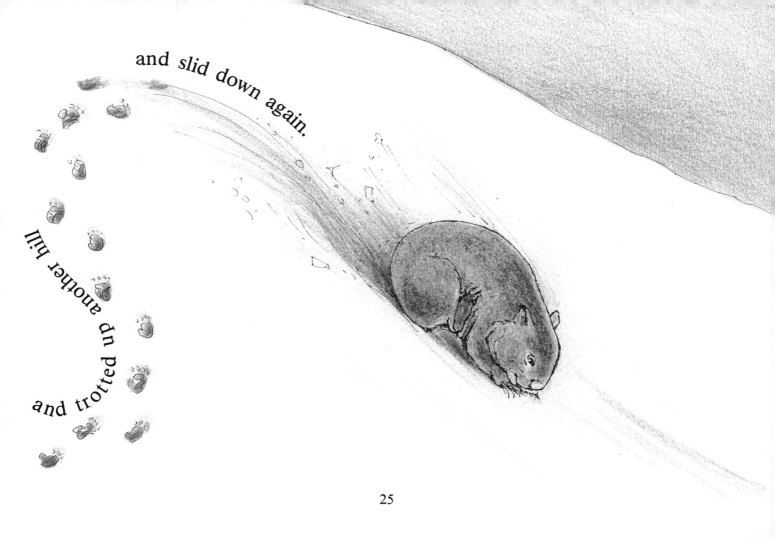

and slid down again.

and trotted up another hill

A farmer and his dog saw her paw prints in the snow
and tried to follow her.
The farmer was angry because wombats
made holes in his fences.

She ran steadily up a hill and slid fast down the other side.

The young wombat was much too fast
for the farmer.
She knew every burrow and dived into one.

The dog followed and tried to bite her
but her skin was too thick.
She thumped upwards
and bashed the dog's head against the roof
of the burrow.
It yelped and ran away.

She sometimes met male wombats
wandering through her feeding grounds.

She growled
and hissed
and chittered
and bit
and chased them away.

When she was two years old,
the time had come for her to have a wombat baby of her own.
When a male came near, she did not chase him away.

Inside a burrow, she lay on her side
and he cuddled up behind her.
They mated. Then she drove him away.

After a month a baby wombat was born
It was the size of a single peanut
   and naked
     and blind.
It crept from its mother's birth canal
and into her pouch.
It fastened on to one of the two teats
and drank its mother's milk . . .

    Another wombat had begun its life.

One wombat lived for 27 years in captivity,
        but nobody knows how long they live in the wild.

Wombats will push through
    swinging gates instead of
      making holes in the farmers' fences.